KU-635-416

Dog at School

by **Katie Dale** and **Gustavo Mazali**

W

FRANKLIN WATTS

LONDON•SYDNEY

It was lunchtime at school.
Mr Jones the head teacher
was in his office.

A dog ran into the playground
and took Dan's football.

Dan chased him.

"Come back, dog," he shouted.

"Mr Jones will be cross."

"Woof," barked the dog.

The dog ran into the school garden.

He jumped on Mr Potts's flowers.

Mr Potts and Dan chased him.

"Come back, dog," they shouted.

"You are muddy.

Mr Jones will be cross."

"Woof, woof," barked the dog.

The dog ran into a classroom.
A jar of water went all over
Ling's painting.

Ling, Mr Potts and Dan chased him.

"Come back, dog," they shouted.

"You are muddy and soggy.

Mr Jones will be cross."

"Woof, woof, woof," barked the dog.

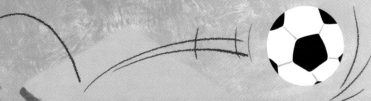

Next, the dog ran into the kitchen.

He took some sausages.

Miss Jenkins the dinner lady,

Ling, Mr Potts and Dan chased him.

"Come back, dog," they shouted.

"You are muddy and soggy

and cheeky.

Mr Jones will be cross."

"Woof, woof, woof, woof,"

barked the dog.

The dog ran towards
the head teacher's office.
"Oh no!" everyone said.

Mr Jones came out of his office.

"What is all this noise?" he shouted.

"WOOF!" barked the dog.

He jumped up

and licked Mr Jones's face.

15

"He's not my dog," said Mr Potts.

"I didn't bring him to school,"
said Miss Jenkins.

"We don't know him,"
said Ling and Dan.

"This is **my** dog," said Mr Jones.

"He lives in my house.

Spot!

What are you doing **in school**?"

Spot went into Mr Jones's office.

"Did you miss me, Spot?"
said Mr Jones.

"Woof!" barked Spot.

19

Story order

Look at these 5 pictures and captions.
Put the pictures in the right order
to retell the story.

Spot went into Mr Jones's office.

Everyone chased the dog.

3

The dog ran into the school garden.

4

The dog licked Mr Jones.

5

The dog ran into a classroom.

Independent Reading

This series is designed to provide an opportunity for your child to read on their own. These notes are written for you to help your child choose a book and to read it independently.

In school, your child's teacher will often be using reading books which have been banded to support the process of learning to read. Use the book band colour your child is reading in school to help you make a good choice. *Dog at School* is a good choice for children reading at Orange Band in their classroom to read independently.

The aim of independent reading is to read this book with ease, so that your child enjoys the story and relates it to their own experiences.

About the book

When a dog runs into the school playground and through the school, everyone is worried that Mr Jones, the head teacher, will be cross. Then the dog runs straight up to Mr Jones and gives him a big lick! But Mr Jones isn't cross at all.

Before reading

Help your child to learn how to make good choices by asking: "Why did you choose this book? Why do you think you will enjoy it?" Look at the cover together and ask: "What do you think the story will be about?" Ask your child to think of what they already know about the story context. Then ask your child to read the title aloud.

Ask: "What do you know about having pets at school? Do dogs usually run through schools?"

Remind your child that they can sound out the letters to make a word if they get stuck.

Decide together whether your child will read the story independently or read it aloud to you.

During reading

Remind your child of what they know and what they can do independently. If reading aloud, support your child if they hesitate or ask for help by telling the word. If reading to themselves, remind your child that they can come and ask for your help if stuck.

After reading

Support comprehension by asking your child to tell you about the story. Use the story order puzzle to encourage your child to retell the story in the right sequence, in their own words. The correct sequence can be found at the bottom of the next page.

Help your child think about the messages in the book that go beyond the story and ask: "Would you like to have a pet come to your school? Why/why not?"

Give your child a chance to respond to the story: "Did you have a favourite part? Why do you think everyone was worried about what Mr Jones would say? What does this tell you about Mr Jones?"

Extending learning

Help your child understand the story structure by using the same sentence patterning and adding different elements. "Let's make up a new story about a pet at school. Which pet shall we choose? What will happen when this pet runs through the school? Who does this pet belong to?"

In the classroom, your child's teacher may be teaching compound nouns, where two words are joined together to make a single noun. There are examples in this book that you could look at with your child, for example: *lunchtime, playground, classroom.*

Franklin Watts
First published in Great Britain in 2017
by The Watts Publishing Group

Copyright © The Watts Publishing Group 2017

Series Editors: Jackie Hamley and Melanie Palmer
Series Advisors: Dr Sue Bodman and Glen Franklin
Series Designer: Peter Scoulding

A CIP catalogue record for this book is
available from the British Library.

ISBN 978 1 4451 5429 9 (hbk)
ISBN 978 1 4451 5430 5 (pbk)
ISBN 978 1 4451 6104 4 (library ebook)

Printed in China

Franklin Watts
An imprint of
Hachette Children's Group
Part of The Watts Publishing Group
Carmelite House
50 Victoria Embankment
London EC4Y 0DZ

An Hachette UK Company
www.hachette.co.uk

www.franklinwatts.co.uk

FSC
www.fsc.org
MIX
Paper from
responsible sources
FSC® C104740

Answer to Story order: 3, 5, 2, 4, 1